HEIDI HECKELBECK

Has a Secret

By Wanda Coven
Illustrated by Priscilla Burris

SCHOLASTIC INC.
New York Toronto London Auckland
Sydney Mexico City New Delhi Hong Kong

No part of this publication may be reproduced, stored in a retrieval system, or transmitted in any form or by any means, electronic, mechanical, photocopying, recording, or otherwise, without written permission of the publisher. For information regarding permission, write to Simon & Schuster Books for Young Readers, an imprint of Simon & Schuster Children's Publishing Division, 1230 Avenue of the Americas, New York, NY 10020.

ISBN 978-0-545-46799-5

12 11 10 9 8 7 6 5 4 3 2   12 13 14 15 16 17/0

Printed in the U.S.A.   40

First Scholastic printing, April 2012

CONTENTS

Chapter 1

GROUCHY

Heidi Heckelbeck woke up in the King-dom of Gloom.

Grouchy Land.

Grumpsville, USA.

Heidi felt like the princess of Crankypants. Because not only was it the first day of school—it was her first day of school EVER.

Heidi had never been to school before. She had always had school at home with her five-year-old brother, Henry. Mom had been their teacher. But starting today Heidi Heckelbeck would be a brand-new second grader at Brewster Elementary.

Mom popped her head into Heidi's room. "Time to get up!" she sang.

"Merg!" growled Heidi.

She flumped her pillow on top of her face. A million questions swirled in her head. What if the teacher was mean? What if she couldn't find her way to the bathroom? What if she sat next to a boy who picked his nose?

Heidi dragged herself out of bed and got dressed. She put on her black jean skirt with her kitty cat top. Then she wiggled into her black-and-white-striped tights and black sneakers. Not even her favorite outfit made her feel cheery. She plodded downstairs.

Mom placed a happy-face pancake in front of Heidi. It had blueberry eyes, a mouth of raspberries, and sausage eyebrows.

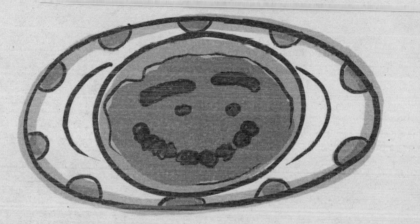

Heidi stuck out her tongue at her pancake.

"It's still smiling," said Henry.

Heidi used her fork to move the food around.

"Not anymore," said Heidi.

"Mom!" yelled Henry. "Heidi made a mad-face pancake!"

Heidi rolled her eyes.

"You know what?" said Henry as he dipped a sausage in syrup. "You

should wear pink. Pink looks friendly."

"Pretty in pink!" added Mom with a wink.

"Wait, what's wrong with the way I look?" said Heidi.

"Uh . . . nothing, really," said Henry.

"It's just that your outfit kind of looks like a Halloween costume. What if you spook the other kids on your first day of school?"

"Har-dee-har-har," said Heidi. But Henry's comment kind of bugged her.

★ ✦ ✳ ◎ ✦

Heidi's dad walked into the kitchen as he fixed his tie.

"Zip-a-dee-doo-dah, zip-a-dee-ay!" he sang. He stopped when he saw Heidi's unhappy face. She was not in a Disneyland mood.

"What's the matter, pumpkin?" asked Dad.

"Nothing," said Heidi. "I just don't want to go to school—EVER. That's all."

Henry dropped his fork.

"Never, ever?" asked Henry. "That means you won't get to have a class pet! Or your own personal desk! Or fire drills."

"Who cares?" said Heidi.

Dad sat down next to Heidi.

"All is well," said Dad. "And all will be well at school too."

"But I want to have school at home with Mom," said Heidi.

"We had a lot of fun," said Mom, "but now it's time to learn from teachers and books at school."

"I can teach myself," said Heidi. "Besides, I like *my* book better."

Mom raised her eyebrows.

"School needs you, Heidi," said Dad. "You're clever and kind."

"And kind of cuckoo," added Henry.

"Trust me," said Dad. "I know you're going to love school. And when you get home, you can be the first to test my brand-new fruit cola formula. I'm thinking of calling it Cherry Zing."

Mr. Heckelbeck worked at a soda pop company called The FIZZ. Heidi loved to try his secret formulas.

Sometimes Heidi came up with her own formulas and shared them with her dad. Tasting a new fruit cola did sound a tiny bit fun.

Mom jingled her car keys. "Time to go," she said cheerfully.

Heidi groaned and slid off of her chair. She put on her black jean jacket and backpack. Then she said her good-byes: "Good-bye, tree fort classroom! Good-bye, backyard cafeteria!"

"You forgot something," said Henry.

"What?" asked Heidi.

"HELLO, SCHOOL!"

And off they went.

Chapter 2

DOUBLE GROUCHY

Heidi wrote her favorite growly word on the foggy car window. *Merg!* She wished the drive to school would never end. She didn't want to learn double-digit addition. She did not feel like making new friends. Heidi squished an old Goldfish cracker into the crumb-filled floor mat. *Crunch*.

Mom parked in the Visitors Only parking spot.

"We're here!" she sang.

Heidi stared at the large brick building. Brewster Elementary looked like a dungeon. Why did it look so creepy? And why did it feel like she had eaten cotton balls for breakfast? And how come the car door felt so heavy?

"Hurry up!" said Henry.

He bounded up the steps and dashed through the door.

Heidi felt like she was wearing Frankenstein shoes. She clumped up the stairs. Mom followed.

The principal, Mr. Pennypacker, greeted them in the main office. He had a tuft of brown hair on either side of his head and no hair in the middle. Heidi thought his hairdo looked like earmuffs.

"I'll take Heidi to second grade," he said. "And my assistant, Mrs. Crosby, will take Henry to kindergarten."

Henry was so lucky. He only had to stay a half day. Heidi thought a half day sounded easy.

"Can I take the bus home, Mom?" begged Henry. "Can I? Can I?"

"Sure," said Mom. "And what about you, Heidi?"

"I want to be picked up."

Mom nodded. Then she gave Heidi and Henry a squeeze and slipped out the door.

Chapter 3

HELLO, MEANIE

Heidi followed Principal Pennypacker down the hall. It smelled like pencils and floor wax.

"You're going to love Brewster Elementary," said the principal.

I doubt it, thought Heidi.

They passed a winter wonderland

mural. It showed penguins sledding, snowboarding, and throwing snow-balls. Heidi thought it looked dumb.

"Do you like sports?" asked Principal Pennypacker.

"Nope," said Heidi.

"How about art?"

"Not really."

"Reading?"

"Kind of."

"What do you like to read?" he asked.

"My special book," said Heidi. "But I forget the name."

"Oh," said the principal.

✦ ✦ ✱ ◎ ✦

When Heidi arrived at her classroom, her teacher came to the door.

"Oh, you must be Heidi," she said. "Welcome!"

Heidi studied the room. She saw a fish tank, a bulletin board about

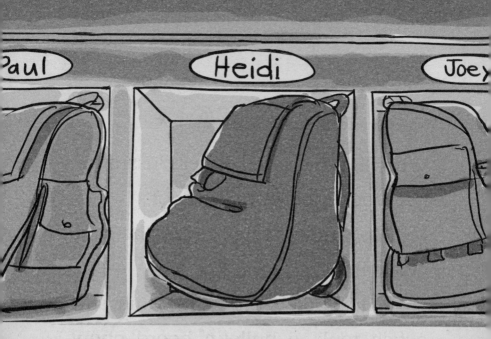

Dr. Martin Luther King Jr., and a reading corner with beanbag chairs.

"I'm Mrs. Wellington," she said. "But everyone calls me Mrs. Welli for short."

Mrs. Welli showed Heidi her cubby and her desk. The cubby had chipped red paint and a sticker with her name on it. Heidi pulled out her pencil case and notebook and stuffed her back-pack into the cubby. She hung her jean jacket on a hook.

Then Heidi sat down at her desk. The lid squeaked when she opened it. The legs rocked when she leaned on

it. It had a number line that went from one through twenty and an alphabet chart on top. The only good thing about it was the shiny name tag. Heidi scooched in her chair.

Mrs. Welli introduced Heidi to the class.

"Wel-come, Hei-di," they all said together.

Someone tapped a pencil.

Heidi looked.

It was a blond-haired girl in a purple ruffly skirt and a polka-dot top.

The girl scrunched her face at Heidi. Then she raised her hand.

"Yes, Melanie?" asked Mrs. Welli.

"Something's smelly, Mrs. Welli," she said with a pinched nose.

The class giggled.

Mrs. Welli clapped her hands. "That's enough, Melanie," she said.

Melanie smiled sweetly. Then she turned and made another mean face at Heidi.

Heidi looked the other way. *Why is this girl being so mean to me?* she wondered. Heidi sniffed her sleeve. *Do I really smell?*

Suddenly another girl, who was two rows up, turned around and looked at Heidi. Heidi braced herself for another prickly glare.

But this time she got a warm, fuzzy smile.

Chapter 4

MEEP! MEEP!

One fuzzy smile did not fix a whole bunch of merg. Heidi sat at her desk and wondered, *Can an eight-year-old drop out of school?* While Heidi thought, she doodled an alien in her new enchanted forest notebook. She drew a thought bubble over her alien's head. *Meep! Meep! Get me off this creepy planet!* thought Heidi.

As she doodled, the teacher wrote homophones on the board. Heidi already knew about homophones. They were words that sounded the same but were spelled differently or had different meanings.

"Okay," said Mrs. Welli to the class. "Pick two sets of homophones and write a sentence for each one. Those of you who would like to share may raise your hand when you're ready."

Heidi looked at the words on the board. She picked two and wrote:

School is a big, fat bore.
Melanie is a mean, nasty boar.

I have a KNOT in my stomach.
I am not coming back to school.

Heidi looked up when she was done. The girl who had smiled at her had her hand up. Mrs. Welli called on her.

"You may come to the front of the classroom, Lucy."

Lucy walked up to the board.

"My words are 'holy' and 'holey,'" said Lucy. "And 'bare' and 'bear.'"

The chalk squeaked as she wrote. Lucy walked back to her desk when she was done. Then Mrs. Welli read Lucy's sentences out loud and underlined each homophone:

<u>Holy</u> Toledo!
I have <u>holey</u> socks!

A <u>bear</u> ate our picnic.
My brother ran down the street <u>bare</u> naked.

The class cracked up the whole time.

"Good work, Lucy!" said Mrs. Welli. Heidi thought Lucy's sentences were pretty good too, but that did not change Heidi's funky mood. She covered her own sentences with her arm so no one would see.

After language arts, Heidi sat through social studies and math. In math, they worked on fact families. *Bo-ring,* thought Heidi. Mom had already taught that at home. Heidi made up her own fact family, only instead of numbers she used words:

Heidi + School = Yuck

Yuck - Heidi = School

Yuck - School = Heidi

Her fact family kind of worked, she thought. At least it had helped her get all the way to lunch. *Just a few more hours and I can go home*, thought Heidi.

Chapter 5

A NEW FRiEND

Lunch.

Ugh.

Heidi had never had lunch in a cafeteria before. She didn't know anybody. She would have to sit all by herself. Double ugh. She grabbed her lunch from her cubby and followed the kids down the hall. Someone shouted her name.

"Heidi! Heidi!"

It was Henry. He waved like crazy from the school bus line.

Heidi gave Henry a *shhhh* face.

Henry ignored her.

"Isn't school FUN?" he said excitedly. "We got to do musical movement and paint decorations for the school play!"

Heidi gave Henry a halfhearted high five and kept walking. He was so happy, it was weird.

The lunchroom smelled like stinky soup. Heidi found an empty table and

sat down on a cold plastic seat. She pulled out her peanut-butter-and-grape-jelly sandwich and chocolate chip cookie. A note was taped to her sandwich. It read:

Smile, Pumpkin!
School will be
great!
Love You!
Mom

The note from Mom made Heidi miss home even more. Not even her favorite sandwich tasted right.

★ ⋆ ✳ ◎ ⋆

"May I sit here?" a girl asked.

It was Lucy. The girl who smiled and wrote funny sentences. Heidi nodded her head up and down.

"My name is Lucy Lancaster," she said.

Heidi nodded again.

"How do you like school so far?" Lucy asked.

Heidi looked at the table.

"That's okay," said Lucy. "It'll get better. So guess what?"

"What?" asked Heidi.

"We have play practice today. Our grade is doing *The Wizard of Oz*."

Gulp. Heidi did not like the sound of a play. The last thing she wanted was to be in the spotlight.

"I'm going to be Auntie Em plus a Munchkin," Lucy went on. "Pretty cool, right?"

"I guess," said Heidi.

Lucy told Heidi who got the best parts.

Soon the bell rang.

"Want to play at recess?" asked Lucy.

Heidi thought that sounded kind of okay. "Sure," she said.

Wow, now Heidi the Alien had a friend.

Meep! Meep!

Chapter 6

BIG TROUBLE

"This is the art room," said Lucy. "Isn't it great?"

Heidi looked around. The art room looked like a children's museum. The walls had paintings of owls and lady-bugs and rocket ships and monsters. Mobiles dangled from the ceiling.

Clay creatures lined the shelves.

"See that bird's nest mobile?" said Lucy. She pointed at the ceiling. "That's mine. It has real birds' eggs inside of it."

Melanie overheard Lucy talking.

"That's right," said Melanie. "Real stinky eggs." She gave Lucy and Heidi a scrunchy face and turned away.

Lucy rolled her eyes. "As I was saying," she said, "you're going to love art."

Heidi stunk at art. She could barely draw a stick figure. She had never worked with clay or made a mobile.

And most of all she did not want to do art anywhere near Melanie. Heidi sat down at a table in the corner. Lucy sat next to her. At each place was a piece of white construction paper and a foam plate with dabs of colored paint. A coffee can full of paintbrushes sat at the middle of the table with two cups of water to dip brushes.

"Smocks on, everyone! Chop-chop!"

said the art teacher as he clapped.

"That's Mr. Doodlebee," whispered Lucy. "He's really nice."

Mr. Doodlebee had a long brown ponytail. He wore a T-shirt with a

swirly design on it, paint-speckled jeans, and red high-tops. Heidi thought he looked like a skateboarder.

"Today we're going to paint self-portraits," said the teacher. "Let's get started. I'll come around to help."

Heidi stared at her paper. *Should I draw my alien self or my regular self?* she wondered. *Is there really any difference?* She dabbed a brush in pale pink paint and drew an oval face. She painted blue eyes with light brown eyelashes. She drew a pointy little nose and a purple line for a mouth. Then she painted strands of red hair.

The teacher came to the table and watched as Heidi painted.

"Nice work," said the teacher. "You must be Heidi. I'm Mr. Doodlebee."

Heidi kept painting.

"I'm here if you need help," said Mr. Doodlebee, and he moved on to another table.

★ ★ ✳ ◎ ★

What Heidi really needed was some brown paint to mix in with the red. She got up and went to the paint station. She pumped a glop of brown

paint from a jar. But when she came back, Melanie was at her place. She had painted a zigzag mouth on Heidi's picture.

"Stop it!" said Heidi.

"What's wrong?" asked Melanie. "I just made your picture look more like you."

Heidi picked up her paintbrush and wiped it across Melanie's smock.

Melanie shrieked and swiped her paintbrush at Heidi. But Melanie missed because Mr. Doodlebee had grabbed her arm in midair.

"Come with me," said Mr. Doodlebee, and he marched Melanie straight to the principal's office.

Heidi crumpled up her self-portrait and dropped it on the table. Melanie Maplethorpe had to be the meanest girl on planet Earth. She felt a tear roll down her cheek. She wiped her eyes with the back of her arm. She could hear kids whispering things.

"Are you okay?" asked Lucy.

"No," said Heidi. "I'm not okay. I want to go home!"

Tears spilled from Heidi's eyes.

When Mr. Doodlebee returned to the classroom, he asked Heidi to come into his office. He gave her tissues and told her that everything would be okay. Heidi felt too embarrassed to say anything. She stayed in his office until the end of art.

Then there was a knock on the door. It was Lucy.

"Hey, Heidi," she said. "I've got good news."

"What?" asked Heidi.

"Melanie got in BIG trouble."

Chapter 7

DRAMA QUEENS

Big mouth.

Big liar.

Big meanie.

"That Melanie is nothing but BIG trouble," said Heidi.

Heidi and Lucy laughed as they walked to play practice. Heidi hadn't

laughed all day. It felt really good.

In the auditorium a round lady with curly orange hair was playing the piano. Heidi recognized the song. It was "Somewhere over the Rainbow."

The girls walked onto the stage and sat at a table. Behind them was a set of the Yellow Brick Road with the Emerald City in the distance. When everyone was seated, the lady stopped playing. Her heels clickety-clacked up the stairs and onto the stage.

"Hello, boys and girls!" said the teacher. "I have your scripts today!" She waved an emerald green script back and forth so everyone could see.

"Melanie and Stanley, please pass these out."

The teacher handed them each a stack of scripts.

A script landed in front of each student.

WUMP!

WUMP!

WUMP!

Melanie paused when she got to
Heidi.

"Mrs. Noddywonks?" said Melanie
sweetly. "Does the new girl get one
too?"

"Yes, dear. Everybody should get
one," said Mrs. Noddywonks.

Melanie dropped a script in front of Heidi. It landed with a thud. Heidi kept her eyes on the table. Then Mrs. Noddywonks called her name.

"Heidi?" she said as she put on her glasses and looked for Heidi. "Heidi Heckelbeck? Did I pronounce your last name correctly?"

Heidi nodded.

"Hello, honey," said Mrs. Noddy-wonks. "Welcome to the wonderful land of Oz! Our play has already been cast, but don't worry, we'll find something fun for you to do."

Phew! thought Heidi. She didn't

have to worry about being in the play. But wait. What was going on? Meanie Melanie was whispering something to Mrs. Noddywonks.

Mrs. Noddywonks nodded and looked at Heidi.

"I have wonderful news, Heidi!" Mrs. Noddywonks said excitedly. "Melanie has found a part for you in the play!"

Heidi's hair stuck straight out of her head—or at least it felt that way. She did not want a part in the play. She did not want to be a flying monkey. She did not want to be a tin girl, a cowardly lion, a scarecrow, or anything else.

"No, thank you, Mrs. Noddywonks," said Heidi. "I would rather *not* be in the play."

"I know how you feel," said Mrs. Noddywonks. "Melanie told me all about it."

"All about what?" asked Heidi.

"About how you feel left out."

"But I want to be left out," said Heidi.

"Hogwash!" said Mrs. Noddywonks.

"Please tell Heidi your idea, Melanie."

Melanie nodded and smiled.

"As Heidi's new friend," began Melanie, "I am happy to say that she will play the role of a scary apple tree in our school play."

"You know the trees I'm talking about," she went on. "The ones in the Haunted Forest."

Everyone looked at Heidi.

She wanted to throw her script at Melanie.

Lucy squished Heidi's foot under the table. "It'll be okay," she whispered.

"Well, then, it's all settled," said Mrs. Noddywonks. She put on her glasses. "Let's practice pages one through sixteen."

Heidi wanted to scream. Melanie thought she was so BIG. She acted like she owned the second-grade. There was only ONE role for that girl: the Wicked Witch. She wouldn't even need to act! But Melanie hadn't gotten the part of the witch. She had gotten Dorothy! Heidi folded her arms.

Talk about UNFAIR. But then Heidi realized something. If Heidi played a scary apple tree and Melanie played Dorothy, then that could mean only one thing. Heidi would get to throw apples at Melanie.

Now, THAT sounded like fun.

Chapter 8

FOUR ANSWERS

Somehow Heidi lived through an entire day of school. But for her, it felt like an entire *year* of school. She wanted a medal, a hug, and a big bowl of peppermint ice cream with hot fudge sauce. Instead, when Mom picked her up, she got to sit next to Henry, who had his finger in his nose.

"That's so gross," said Heidi.

"What?" said Henry. "Boogers taste great."

"Double gross," said Heidi.

"Did you miss me?" said Henry.

"No," said Heidi.

"Well, I missed you all afternoon," said Henry. "It's boring without you."

"You're weird," said Heidi. "But thanks, bud."

Mom smiled in the rearview mirror.

"So," said Mom, "how was your first day of school?"

Now *that* was a juicy question. Heidi thought of four answers. She could:

1. remain silent

2. scream without stopping

3. explode

4. tell it like it was

Heidi chose answer number four.

"I hated being new," said Heidi. "I felt like an alien all day."

"That's so cool!" said Henry. "What planet are you from?"

"Planet I-Hate-School," said Heidi.

"Never heard of it," said Henry.

"It's awful," said Heidi. "It has a mean-girl leader named Melanie."

"Does she smell?" said Henry. "Because if she smells, you could call her Princess Smell-a-nie."

"Worse," said Heidi. "She said that *I* smell!"

"Wow," said Henry. "She must have a smelly problem."

"Enough smelly talk," said Mom. "I'm sure Melanie didn't mean it."

Of course she meant it, thought Heidi. The name Princess Smell-a-nie was perfect. All Melanie needed was a stinky crown on top of her head.

Chapter 9

ZiNG!

When Heidi got home, Dad was in the
kitchen. He had two plastic bottles
filled with dark liquid on the table.
One was labeled SAMPLE NUMBER 1, and
the other was labeled SAMPLE NUMBER 2.
There was also a bottle of water and a
stack of mini paper cups.

"She's home! My big school girl

is home!" said Dad. Dad gave Heidi
a great big squeeze. She managed a
small smile.

"Are you ready?" asked Dad.

"Ready," said Heidi.

Dad had on his white lab coat. He
set out two cups and then rubbed his
hands together for the big moment.

"Welcome to the Heckelbeck Taste-Testing Laboratory," he said. "As you can see, we have two mystery drinks to choose from today. Please sample one, followed by a glass of water. Then sample the second one. Do not. I repeat. *Do not* make yummy faces *or* yucky faces during the taste test. We

do not want to sway the other tasters."

Dad poured a cup of dark fizzy liquid and a cup of water. He placed both of them in front of Heidi.

"My trusty assistant, Heidi, will go first," said Dad. "Remember, *no* faces!"

Heidi took a sip of the soda. She felt the tingle of the bubbles on her tongue. It had a nice cherry flavor to

it. She set down the cup and sipped some water.

"Now for sample number two," said Dad. He poured the second mystery liquid and handed it to Heidi.

Heidi slowly sipped it. *Wow-wee!* she thought, trying not to let the wow-wee show in her face. This soda had a super-tingly, super-zingy cherry flavor. She set down the cup and sipped some water. Then Mom and Henry took their turns.

"Okay, let's hear from taste-tester number one," said Dad.

"I choose sample number two," said Heidi.

"Taste-tester number two?" asked Dad.

"I pick number two also," said Henry.

"Taste-tester number three?"

"Number two," said Mom.

Dad pumped his fists in the air.

"I'm happy to say that the taste test was a success!" said Dad. "Cherry Zing is the winner!"

Dad looked so happy. He worked so hard on his soda formulas. He wanted them to be the best. Heidi was very proud of him.

"Thanks for your help, guys," said Dad. "So, Heidi, how was your first day of school?"

Oh no, thought Heidi. *Not THAT again*. She felt the fun drain right out of her body. *Drooooooop*.

"Going to school was absolutely, positively the worst thing I've ever done in my life," said Heidi.

"Worse than fabric shopping with your mother?" asked Dad.

"Way worse," said Heidi. "I felt like a complete doofus all day. I just don't fit in at school."

All the yucky feelings of the day bubbled up all over again. Heidi felt awful. She ran upstairs to her room and slammed the door.

Chapter 10

SMELL-A-NiE

Heidi kicked off her shoes and flopped onto her bed. She buried her face in her pillow. Maybe she could stay in bed the rest of her life. That sounded perfect.

Heidi heard the doorknob turn. It was Mom. She came in and sat down on the bed beside Heidi.

"Pretty yucky day, huh?" said Mom.

"Yup," said Heidi in a muffled-pillow voice.

"I know how you feel," said Mom. "It happened to me too."

Heidi rolled over and looked at her mother.

"It did?" questioned Heidi. "When?"

"In grade school," said Mom. "Some of the girls in my class thought I was—you know—different."

"Well, we *are* different," said Heidi. "So, what did you do?"

"I made two really good friends,

and then the mean girls didn't bug me as much."

Heidi sighed.

"You know what I wish?" said Heidi. "I wish I could just be my real self. Why can't I just be a—"

Before Heidi could finish, Henry burst into the room. He had on Mom's high heels and a pair of glasses perched on the end of his nose. He had an open book in his hand.

"Wanna play school?" asked Henry. "We can both be the teachers and my stuffed animals can be the students."

"Not in the mood," said Heidi.

"But I already set up all the stuffed animals on chairs and everything," said Henry. "They're ready to learn!"

"Maybe later," said Heidi.

"Why? Are you still upset about that Smell-a-nie girl?" asked Henry.

"Pretty much," said Heidi.

"Well, I have an idea," said Henry.

"Shoot," said Heidi.

"When Smell-a-nie talks to you, pretend that she has a pair of under-wear on her head," said Henry. "Then she won't seem so scary."

"You are a total Froot Loop," said Heidi.

"Who knows? It might work," said Mom. "But one thing I can promise is that school will get better. Now, who's up for an after-school snack?"

"Cookies?" asked Henry.

"Why not?" said Mom.

Henry raced out the door.

Mom got up and looked at Heidi.

"Uh . . . I'll be down in a sec," said Heidi. A brilliant idea had just popped into her head.

"Okay," said Mom.

THE SECRET!

Once Mom and Henry were gone, Heidi shut the door. Then she lay down on her stomach and pulled her keepsake box out from under her bed. It was bejeweled with rainbow gems and glitter. Heidi undid the silver latch and opened the box. She pulled out a golden medallion on a long

chain. In the middle of the medallion was the letter *W* woven into another *W*. Heidi slipped the medallion over her head. It hung all the way to her lap. She held it in one hand and studied it. Heidi traced the *W* with her finger. A big smile bloomed on her face. Her idea was beautiful. And

wicked. But before starting she would need a snack. She stuck the medallion back into the box and ran downstairs.

"Mom, can I have some cookies?"
asked Heidi. "I need some energy to
do my homework."

"Coming right up!" said Mom. She put two chocolate chip cookies on a plate.

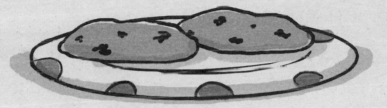

"Does that mean you're going back to school?" asked Henry.

"Yup," said Heidi. "Your underwear trick was just what I needed."

"Really?" asked Henry.

"No," said Heidi.

Heidi ate her cookies, gave Mom a

big hug, and went back upstairs.

Mom almost dropped the milk jug.

"Whoa," said Mom to Henry. "What just happened here?"

Henry shrugged.

As soon as Heidi got back to her room, she pulled out her keepsake box again. This time she pulled out an old worn black leather book. The title on the cover read *Book of Spells*. She opened the book. The first page had a list of fancy signatures. Above the signatures it said *"The Witches of Westwick."* Heidi flipped through the pages. She stopped when she came

to the one that read: *"How to Make Someone Forget."*

"Perfect!" Heidi said to herself with a smile. "Let's see what happens when Princess Smell-a-nie forgets her lines in the play. . . ."

Heidi folded her arms.

One thing's for sure, thought Heidi. *I'm not going to forget who I am. I'm Heidi Heckelbeck, and I'm a WITCH!*